To: Our Favorite Nephews

From: Auntie Laurie,

Uncle David &  Georgie

2022

# The Itchy-saurus

## Rosie Wellesley

STERLING CHILDREN'S BOOKS
New York

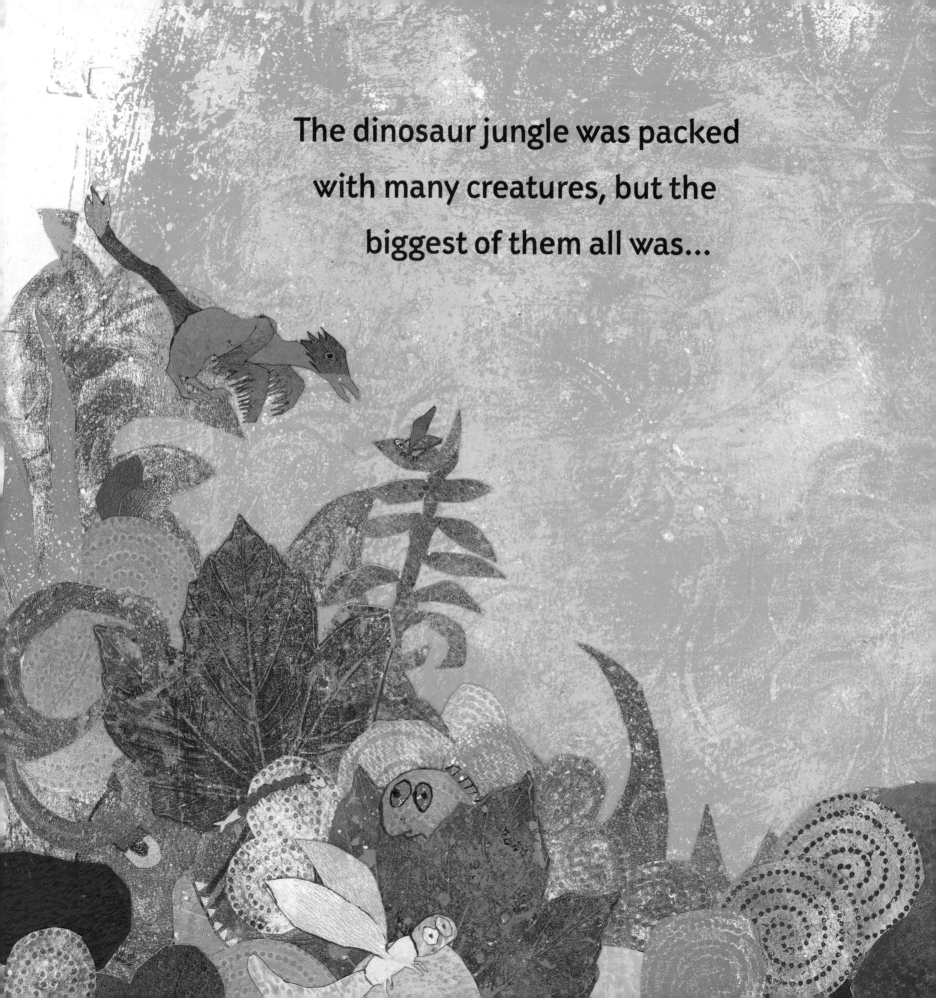

The dinosaur jungle was packed
with many creatures, but the
biggest of them all was...

# Tyrannosaurus Rex.

T Rex liked to roar and stomp and tear
about the place.

He snacked on squishy jungle beasts,
and he was always hungry.

But he tried hard to be kind and calm,
and when the day was done he would
doze beneath the puzzle tree and watch
dragonflies fly by.

Until, one day, his skin began to change.

Where he had once been nice and green,
his scales turned red and hot.

Where he had once been smooth and sleek,
he became all dry and crackly.

His arms began to itch.
His legs began to itch.

He scratched and scratched, but his little arms just couldn't scratch all over.

T Rex now was **angry**.

Where he could scratch,
the rash got worse
and where he couldn't,
it drove him *wild*.

He chased. He bit.
He forgot to ever be kind.

ROOOOOAAARI

He became the biggest, meanest, most DANGEROUS dinosaur in the jungle.

RRR!

One day Doc Bill (the platypus) heard T Rex's fury.

Bill was small and squishy, but he was also brave. He liked making healing potions, and he knew what he must do.

He must go and find this **angry dinosaur.**

As Bill searched, to give him strength,
he sang his magic potion song:

"Hubble bubble, hubble bubble,

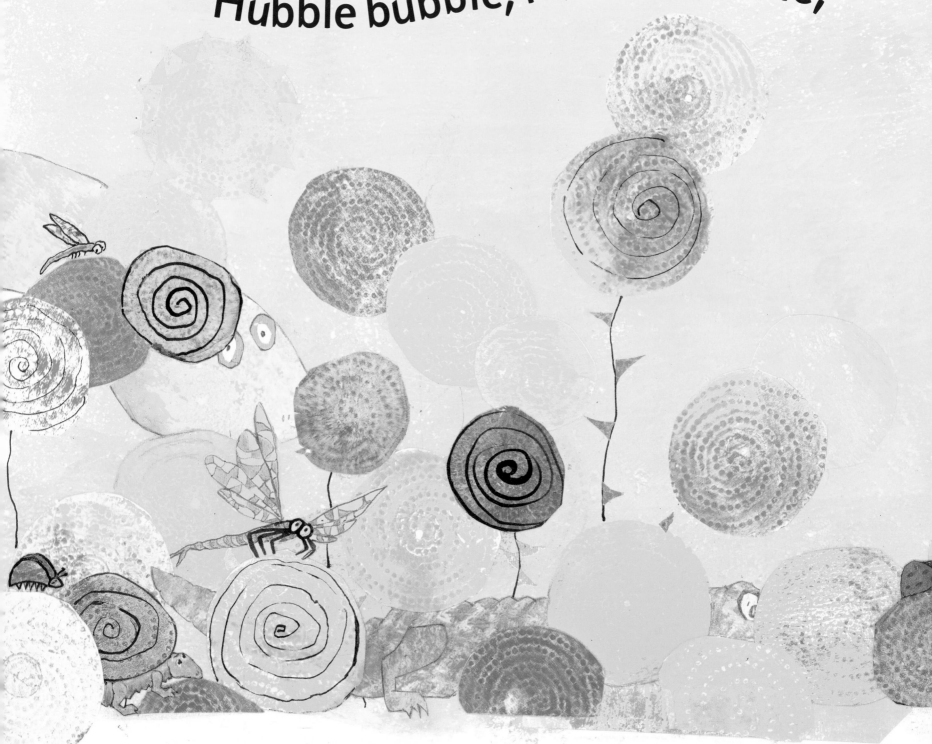

magic potion stir, stir, stirrrrr..."

Finally, Bill found T Rex beside the puzzle tree.

He looked *miserable.*

Bill coughed politely.

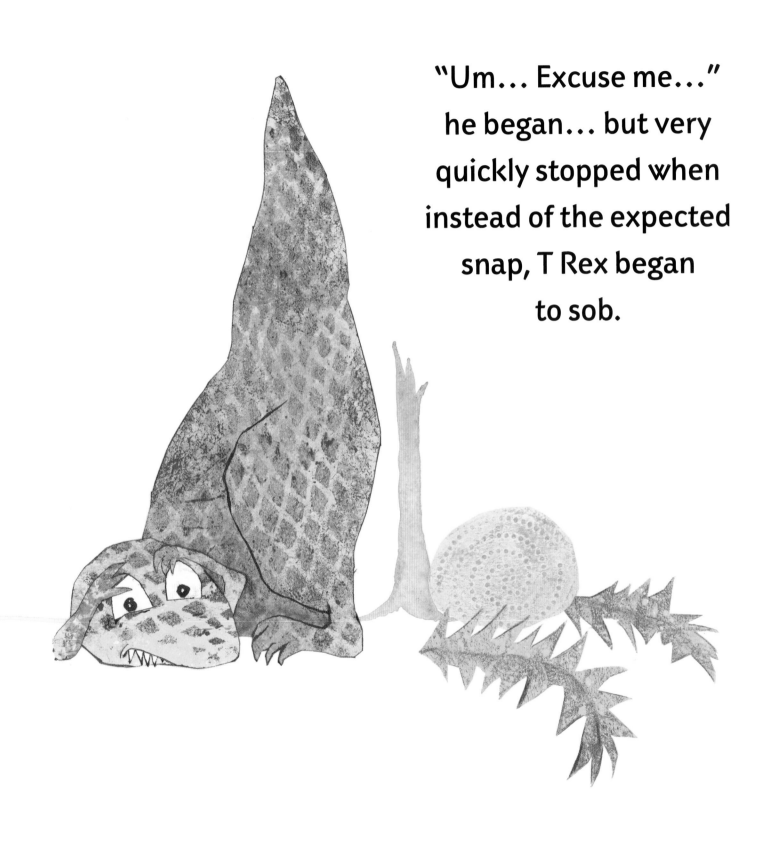

"Um... Excuse me..." he began... but very quickly stopped when instead of the expected snap, T Rex began to sob.

**"What has happened to me?"** wailed T Rex,

"I cannot sleep, I cannot EAT!
I cannot roar and stomp about.

"Because of this red itchy rash all I
can do is scratch, scratch, scratch.

"I'm no Tyrannosaurus,
I... am... an...

ITCHY-SAURUS!"

"Don't worry, Itchy," said Doc Bill.

"It is just T-Rex-zema.

"I can help, but there'll be rules:

1. No biting.
2. **No** stomping.
3. **No** scratching!

"And please be patient."

T Rex nodded quietly.

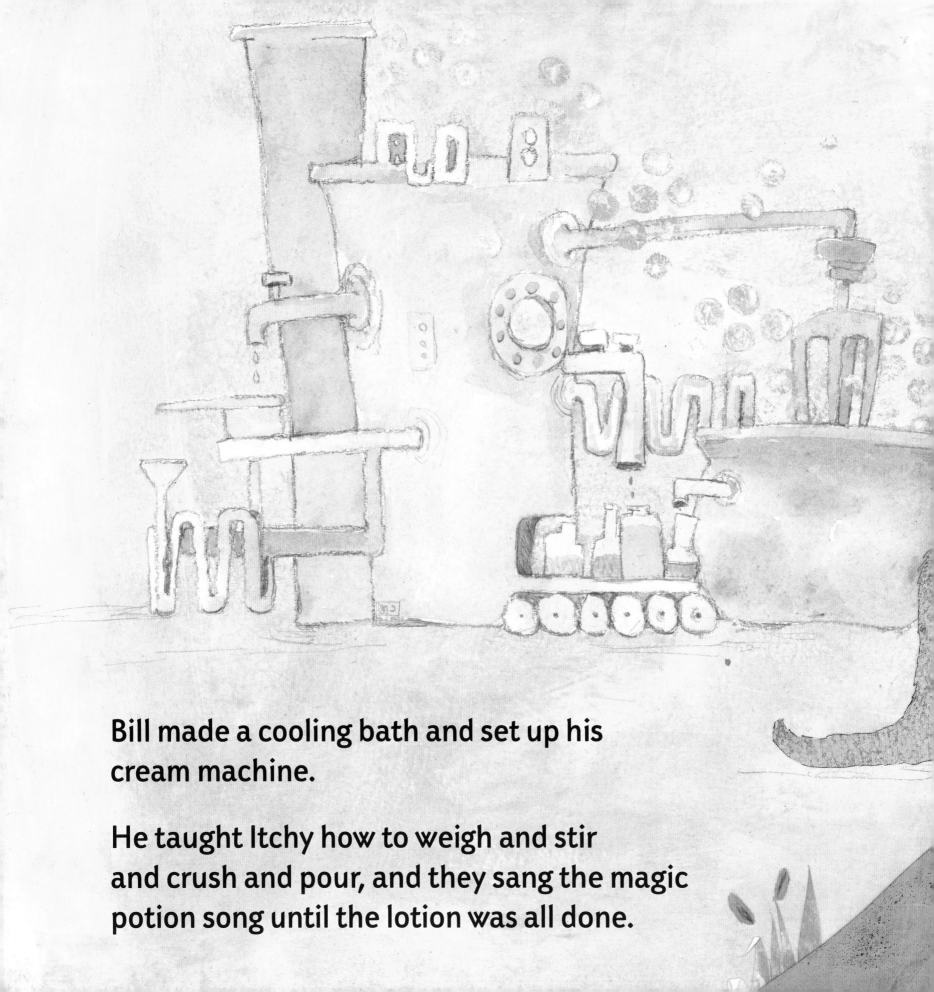

Bill made a cooling bath and set up his
cream machine.

He taught Itchy how to weigh and stir
and crush and pour, and they sang the magic
potion song until the lotion was all done.

"This is very NICE cream," said Bill.

"Very **ice cream?**" asked Itchy, hopefully.

Bill spread the cream all over
Itchy and tucked him up in bed.

For the first time in ages,
the dinosaur slept.

The next day, after more cream,
Itchy waited to feel better.

"I still want to **scratch**," he muttered grumpily.

"You need
distracting,"
said Doc Bill.

So Itchy was taught
to collect wood,
find ingredients,
and tend to sick
jungle creatures.

At bedtime, after cream again, Doc Bill read him stories about a nice dinosaur who roared and stomped but was a **vegetarian**.

Itchy started to have fun.

Itchy forgot
to scratch.

After bath and Nice Cream Time, Itchy showed Bill how to roar and stomp.

**"No biting!"**
reminded Bill.

"Just pretending," muttered Itchy.

Then finally one morning,
T Rex looked down
at his skin.

It wasn't **red.**
It wasn't **itchy.**

He didn't want to scratch.
He felt his **roar** and
**stomp** return.

He looked at Doc.
He felt… he felt…

**hungry**.

He came in close. He **bared his teeth... and...**

"Thank you!" he said.

During the time of the dinosaurs there lived steropodons, ancestors of the duck-billed platypus of today. There were also dragonflies and monkey puzzle trees.

Although we do not know if dinosaurs had eczema, 20% of children do. The National Eczema Association is a useful place for more information.

**To all children with eczema, especially Tobin.**

Special thanks to the patients—children and parents—at the St Andrews Health Centre in Tower Hamlets, London, for your ideas and input into the story. Also to the DIY health team (Clara, Sue, and Emma). It could not have been made without you.

Thanks also to the Wellcome Trust for their funding and patience. To Jean Robinson from the Royal London Hospital, who has taught me so much about eczema and Mapledene Children's Centre in Hackney, for their help and enthusiasm.

STERLING CHILDREN'S BOOKS
New York

An Imprint of Sterling Publishing Co., Inc.
1166 Avenue of the Americas
New York, NY 10036

Text and illustrations © 2018 Rosie Wellesley

First published in the United Kingdom in 2018 by Pavilion Children's Books, 43 Great Ormond St, London WC1N 3HZ

.

ISBN 978-1-4549-3294-9

Distributed in Canada by Sterling Publishing
c/o Canadian Manda Group, 664 Annette Street
Toronto, Ontario M6S 2C8, Canada

For information about custom editions, special sales, and premium and corporate purchases,
please contact Sterling Special Sales at 800-805-5489 or specialsales@sterlingpublishing.com.

Manufactured in China
Lot #:
2 4 6 8 10 9 7 5 3 1
09/18

sterlingpublishing.com